GLEN ARDEN SCHOOL LIBRARY

PETS WITHOUT HOMES

BY CAROLINE ARNOLD
PHOTOGRAPHS BY RICHARD HEWETT

CLARION BOOKS
Ticknor & Fields/A Houghton Mifflin Company/New York

Clarion Books
Ticknor & Fields, a Houghton Mifflin Company

Text copyright © 1983 by Caroline Arnold
Photographs copyright © 1983 by Richard Hewett
All rights reserved.

Printed in the U.S.A.

Library of Congress Cataloging in Publication Data
Arnold, Caroline.
    Pets without homes.
    Summary: Text and photos present an animal shelter which cares for lost pets and also offers other community services.
    1. Animals, Treatment of— Juvenile literature.
2. Pets—Juvenile literature. [1. Animals—Treatment.
2. Pets] I. Hewett, Richard, ill. II. Title.
HV4708.A76 1983   636.08′3   83-2106
ISBN 0-89919-191-6

Y 10 9 8 7 6 5 4

    We want to give special thanks to everyone at the Santa Monica, California Animal Shelter for their time and cheerful cooperation. In particular we want to thank Officer Terrie Lee and Director John Sanchez, and the officers, kennel aides, and volunteers.
    We also want to thank the children and teachers of the Santa Monica Assistance League School for their enthusiastic participation.
    Lastly, we want to give thanks to Buffy and Max, the stars of our story.

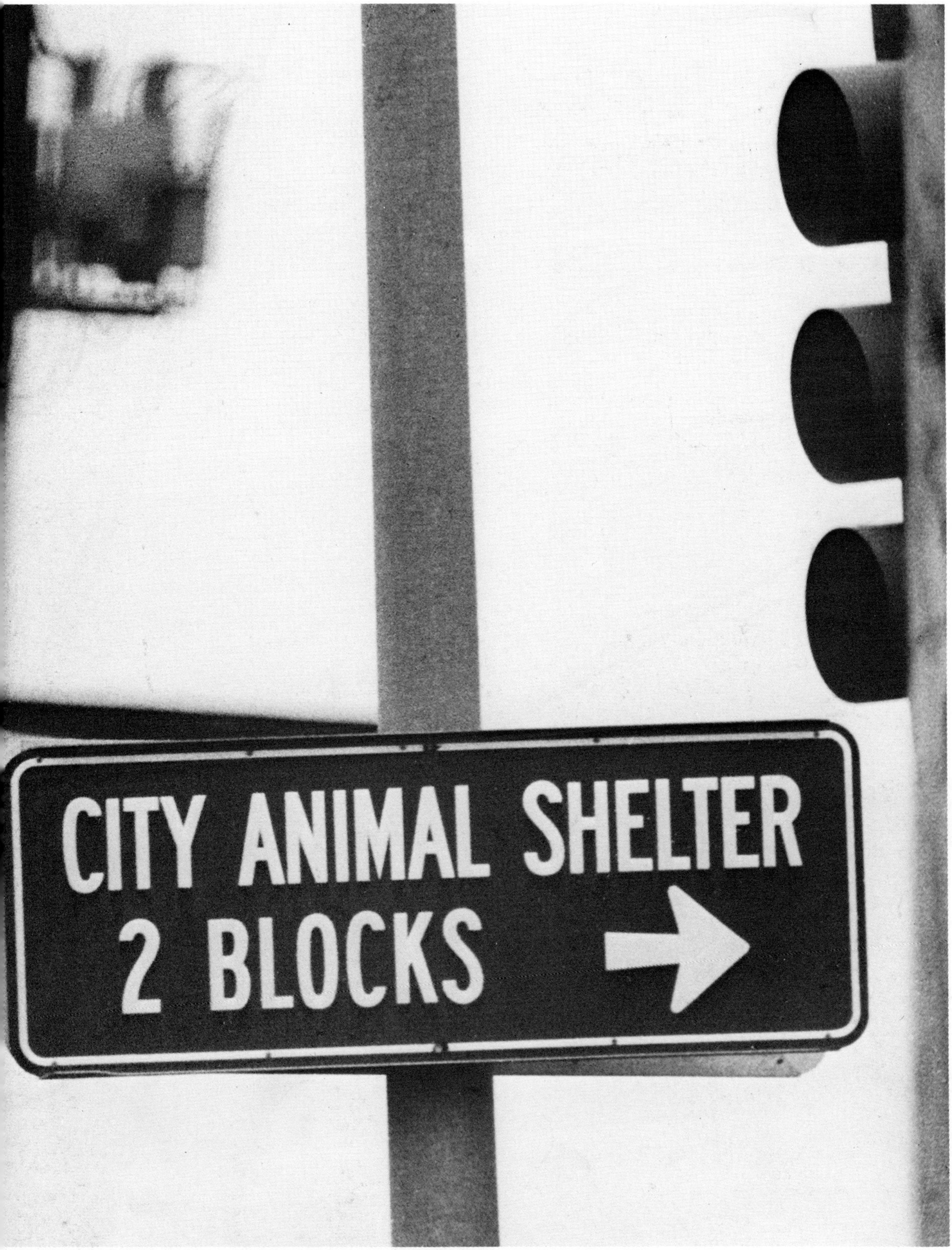
CITY ANIMAL SHELTER
2 BLOCKS

Buffy was a lost, lonely, and hungry puppy when Officer Terrie Lee found him. No one she asked knew where he belonged.

And there was no tag on his collar showing the name or the telephone number of his owner. So Officer Lee picked up Buffy. She would put him in her truck and take him to the city animal shelter.

Officer Lee works for the department of animal control in her city. Every day she and the other animal control officers help animals like Buffy. At the shelter they would take care of Buffy until his owner came for him. If his owner did not come, they would try to find him a new home.

Sometimes officers find animals that are hurt or sick. Then they try to help them get well.

Veterinarians, doctors who treat animals, sometimes work at shelters. But at other shelters, sick animals are taken out to a veterinarian's office. Officer Lee decided to take Buffy to a veterinarian's office before going back to the shelter.

The veterinarian checked Buffy all over. "This dog is not sick," he said. "But he's hungry and needs a warm, dry place to sleep. He should be fine after a day or two at the shelter."

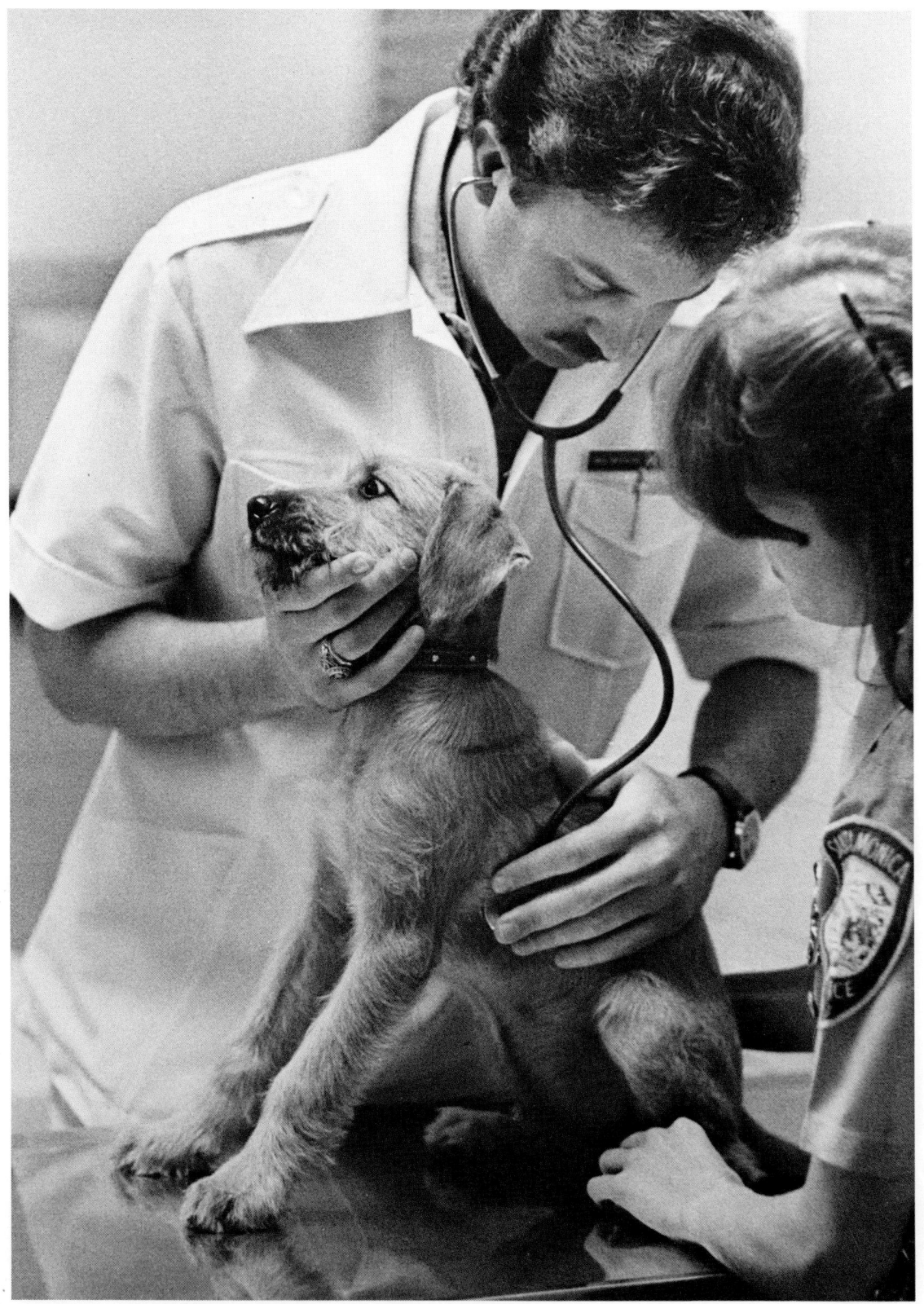

At the animal shelter, Officer Lee took Buffy and the other dog she had found into the office so the dogs could be registered. First she added them to the list of animals that had come to the shelter during the year. Buffy was puppy number 1527. Officer Lee also filled out a card for Buffy. The card showed that he was a tan-colored, male dog about three months old. It said that he was wearing a collar. It also said when and where Buffy was found.

People who are looking for a lost pet often call the animal shelter. The registration card helps the people at the shelter to know if Buffy is the lost dog someone may be looking for.

13

A copy of the card would be put on Buffy's cage. Then people visiting the shelter could read it too.

Officer Lee wrote Buffy's number on a plastic collar. Now no one would be able to confuse Buffy with any other dog in the shelter. Every animal there must wear an identification collar.

Many animal shelters give vaccinations to the animals that come there. The vaccinations help keep the animals healthy. Buffy was given vaccinations for distemper and some other common diseases in dogs.

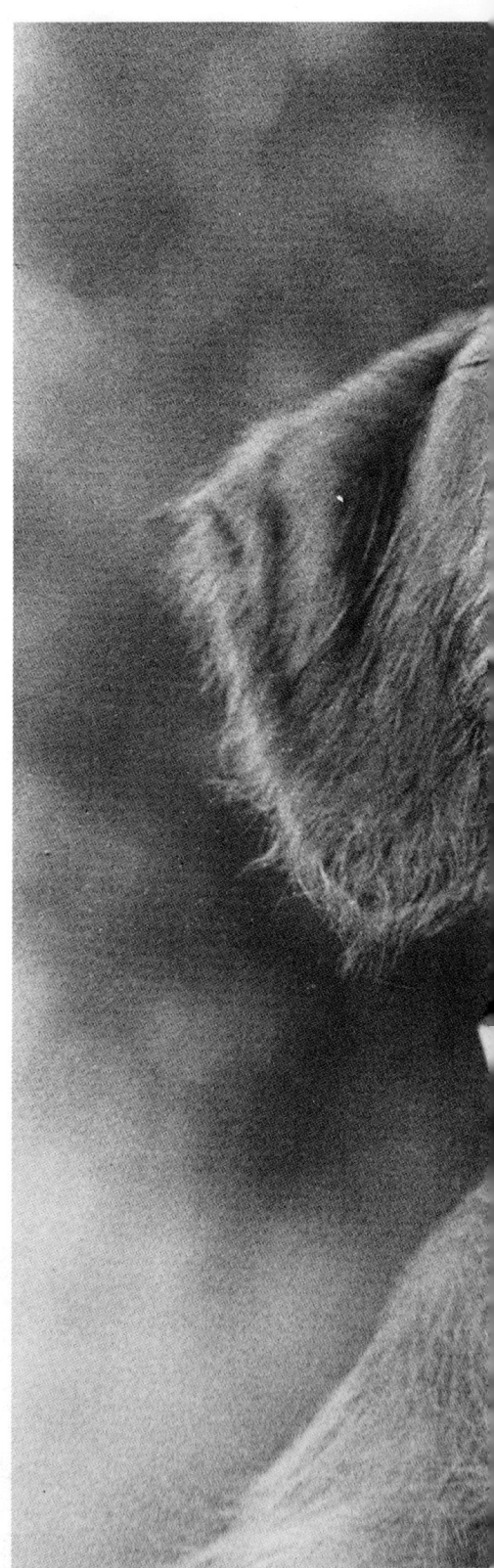

Buffy was now ready to go to the kennel part of the shelter. Officer Lee found an empty cage and opened the door. This cage would be Buffy's new home for the next week or so. He would wait there for his owner to claim him. If Buffy's owner did not come in a week, then Buffy could be adopted by someone else.

Inside Buffy's cage were a pail of water and a bowl of food. A bench on the wall could be used for sleeping. In hot weather, Buffy could go under the bench to get some shade. This part of Buffy's cage was outdoors. Buffy could walk through a small door to go to the inside part of his cage. At night all the animals stayed indoors. But during the day they could go back and forth.

All the other dogs in the kennel began to bark when they saw Buffy. Some of them were strays like Buffy. But some wore tags or licenses. The dogs with identification were waiting for their owners to come get them.

An officer often picks up a dog with a tag or license. Someone at the shelter tries to call the owner or writes the owner a letter. Then the owner will know where to find his or her pet. The owner must pay a fine before taking the pet home. In most cities it is against the law to let your dog run loose.

Loose dogs can knock over garbage cans or dig up people's gardens. They can also get hurt. A dog does not know to cross the street at the corner or to wait for a green light. And sometimes dogs bite people. It is hard to tell if a stray animal will be friendly, so animal control officers tell people to leave an animal they don't know alone. The officers are trained to approach and handle stray animals safely.

If a dog bites someone, an animal control officer checks to make sure the dog has had a rabies vaccination. Rabies is a dangerous disease that can be given by animal bites. In most places dogs must have a rabies vaccination before getting a license. Because of this law, most dogs are now protected against rabies and the disease has become rare.

Not all animals that come to the shelter are strays. Some are brought in by their owners. Max is a cat that was brought to the shelter because his owner was moving. His owner was sad to part with Max. But the rule in the new apartment building was No Pets Allowed. Max's owner had to pay a small fee before the shelter would take Max. The money would help pay for Max's care.

First Max was registered. Then he was put into a cage in the cat kennel. The card on the front of his cage said that Max could be adopted right away. If an owner brings an animal to the shelter, the animal does not have to wait to be adopted.

Max's card also showed that he had been neutered. A male animal that has been neutered has had a simple operation to prevent him from being a father. Female animals are spayed to prevent them from having young. Sometimes animal shelters have low-cost clinics where pets can be spayed or neutered. In some states, all cats at shelters must be spayed or neutered before they can be adopted.

Spaying or neutering is important because a dog or cat can have several litters each year. And each litter can have many puppies or kittens. Thousands of puppies and kittens are born every hour of every day. Most of them do not find homes. Many of these pets without homes end up at animal shelters.

From his cage Buffy could watch people go in and out of the shelter. He could also watch the people working at the shelter. Each time Buffy heard his cage door open, he jumped up to see who it was. Maybe it would be his owner. But each time it was only the kennel aide.

Kennel aides feed the animals and keep them clean. Each morning they hose out the dog cages. The steaming hot water washes away odors and germs. Then they spray the cages with disinfectant. The dogs stay outside while the insides of their cages are being cleaned. Then they go inside when the outsides are being cleaned. Each day the kennel aides also put fresh newspaper and a clean box of litter in each cat cage.

GLEN ARDEN SCHOOL LIBRARY

Puppies like Buffy need to run about and play. Sometimes the kennel aides give toys to the dogs. Good toys for puppies are balls, rubber rings and even old rags. Puppies have growing teeth and need to chew things. Big dogs at the shelter are often put in long cages to run and exercise.

The cats and kittens at the shelter need exercise too. They go to a large play area. The play area has cubbyholes, scratching posts, and other things cats like.

People often go to animal shelters to look for a lost pet. They also go there to look for a new pet. Most people want to adopt a cat or a dog. But animal shelters often have other kinds of animals too. They may have rabbits, hamsters, birds, and fish. Shelters sometimes even have chickens, horses, donkeys, or sheep. Many kinds of animals can be good pets.

The people who came to Buffy's shelter would often stop by Buffy's cage and talk to him. "What a cute puppy!" they would say. But none of the people who came was Buffy's owner.

Then one day Buffy's cage door opened. Was it Buffy's owner at last? No. It was the kennel aide with another puppy. Now Buffy had a playmate. The new puppy was about the same size as Buffy. Like Buffy she had been lost. She was waiting for her owner, too.

A week went by, and Buffy's owner still did not come to get him. Maybe Buffy's owner no longer wanted him. Maybe Buffy's owner had moved away and left him behind. Sometimes people turn their pets loose when they do not want them anymore. They hope that someone else will find them and take care of them. This does not always happen. Often these animals go hungry or get hit by cars. Buffy was lucky that he was found and brought to the shelter. Now, because his owner did not claim him, Buffy could be adopted.

Like the other officers, Terrie Lee sometimes works in the animal shelter office. She answers the telephone. She helps people to find lost pets or to adopt a new pet. She also sells dog licenses. In her city every dog must wear a license. If a dog does not have a license, the owner must pay a fine.

Usually Officer Lee spends most of her day away from the shelter. But each day she would stop by Buffy's cage before she went out. "Hello," she would say and pat Buffy on the nose.

Then Officer Lee would go out on patrol in the animal shelter truck.

Part of the time, she would look for other stray or lost animals. Sometimes she had to give tickets to people walking dogs without leashes. Sometimes she would check complaints about barking dogs or dog bites. Once she was called to move a bird nest that was causing problems in a shopping center.

Officer Lee also visits pet stores to make sure that the animals are being well cared for. The animal control department is a part of the police department in Officer Lee's city. Officer Lee spends her day enforcing laws that have to do with animals in the city.

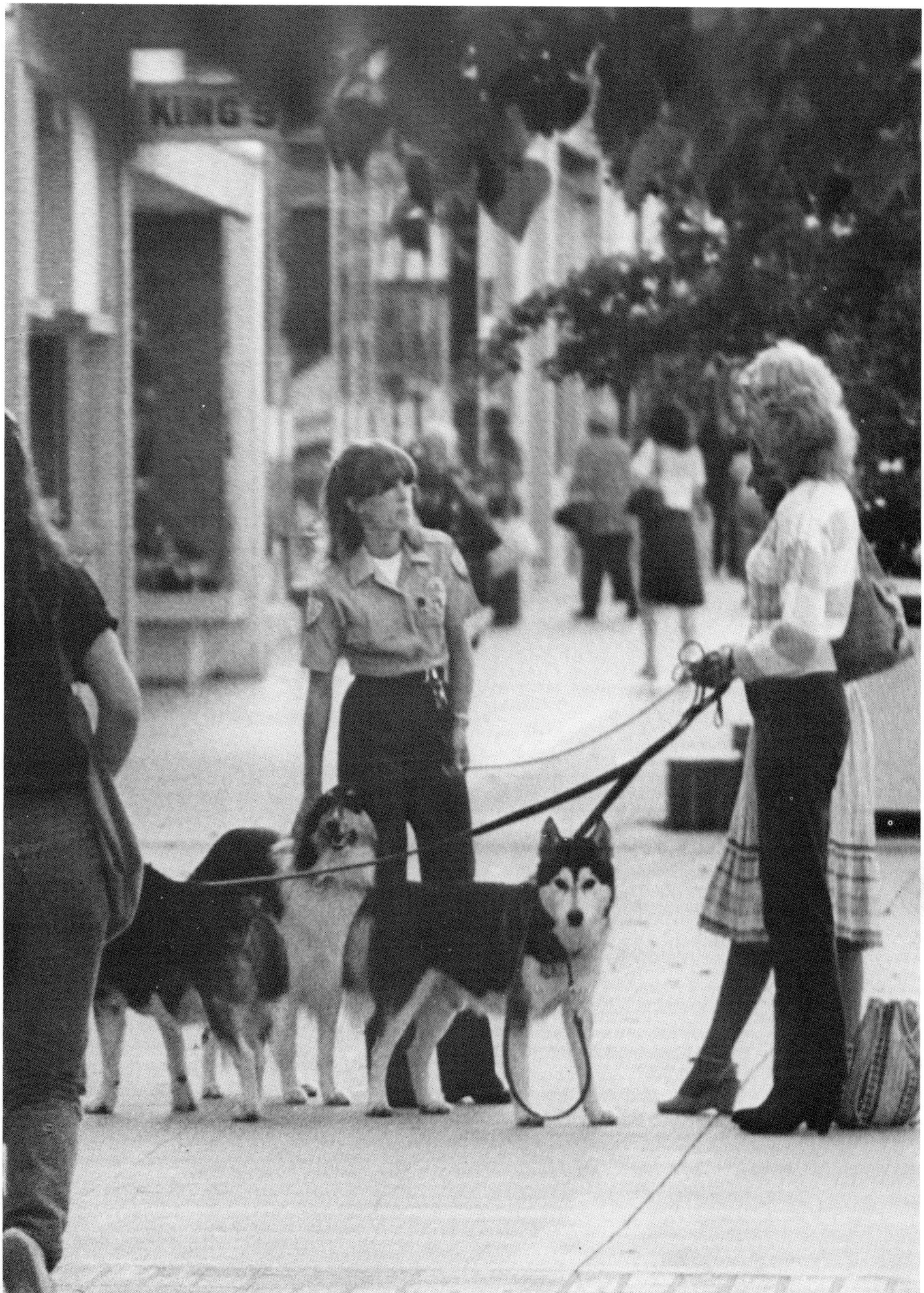

Officer Lee tries to help people learn more about animals and how to care for them. If everyone took good care of his or her animals, there would be less need for animal shelters.

One morning Officer Lee took Buffy and Max out of their cages and put them into her truck. In the truck she also had two kittens and a squirrel. She was taking all of them to visit a school.

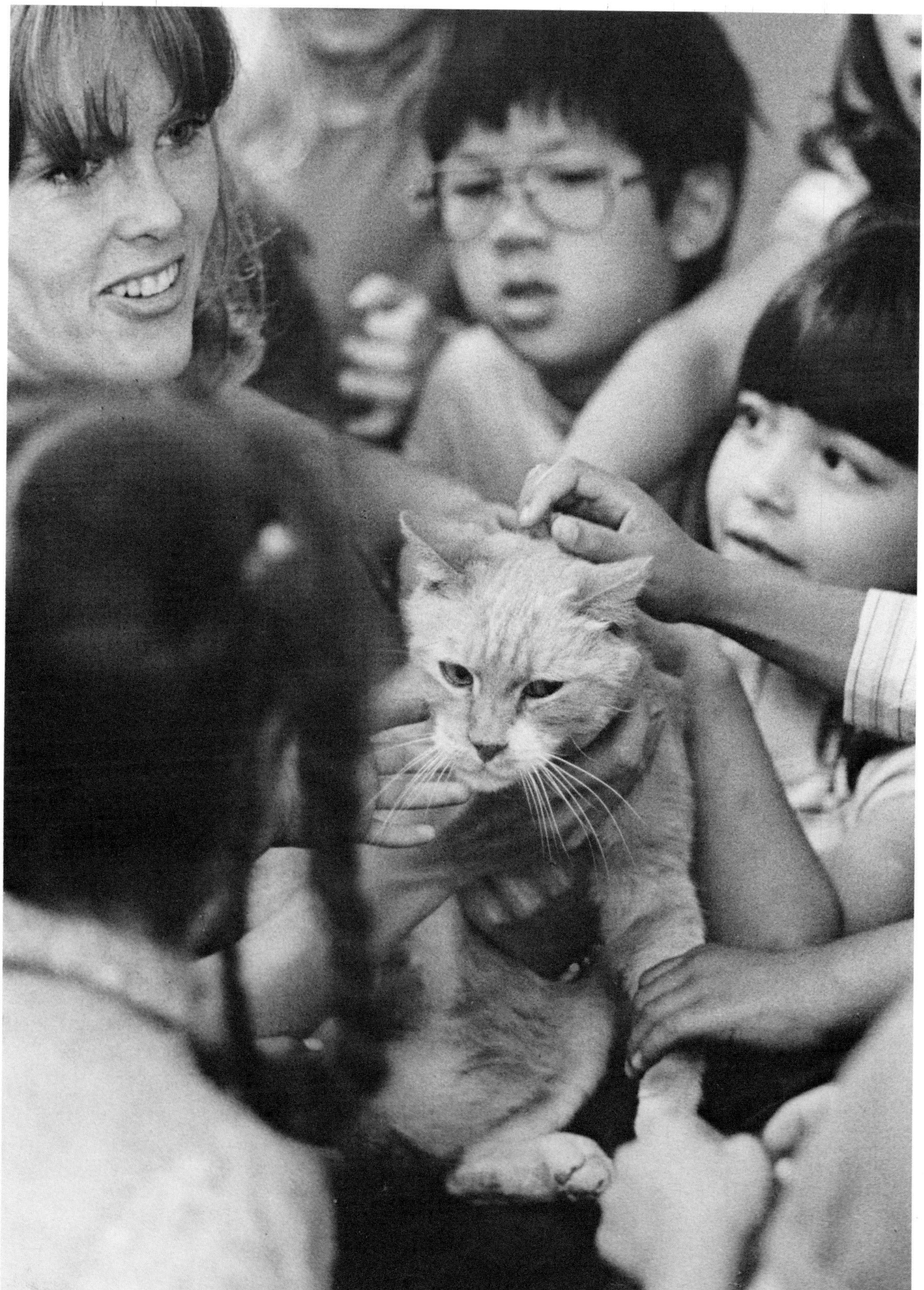

Officer Lee talked to the children at the school about pet care and safety. All pets need food, water, and a place to sleep. They need to be kept clean. And they need a place to exercise.

Pets also need to learn good behavior. Dogs should

not bark when left alone. They should not dig up the neighbor's garden. They should learn to come when called and to walk on a leash.

Cats should learn not to scratch the furniture. Cats can also learn to use a litter box.

Each child at the school had a chance to hold or pet the animals.

The squirrel at the shelter had once been a pet. Officer Lee explained that wild animals do not make good pets. They may be cute when they are young. But as they grow older, they lose their tameness. In most places, it is against the law to keep wild animals. They can be dangerous and can carry diseases.

Wild animals such as raccoons and opossums sometimes cause trouble in the city. Animals like these can learn that it is easier to knock over garbage cans for food than to find food in the wild. Animal control officers often have to catch these animals. Then they take them to a wild place far from the city and let them go.

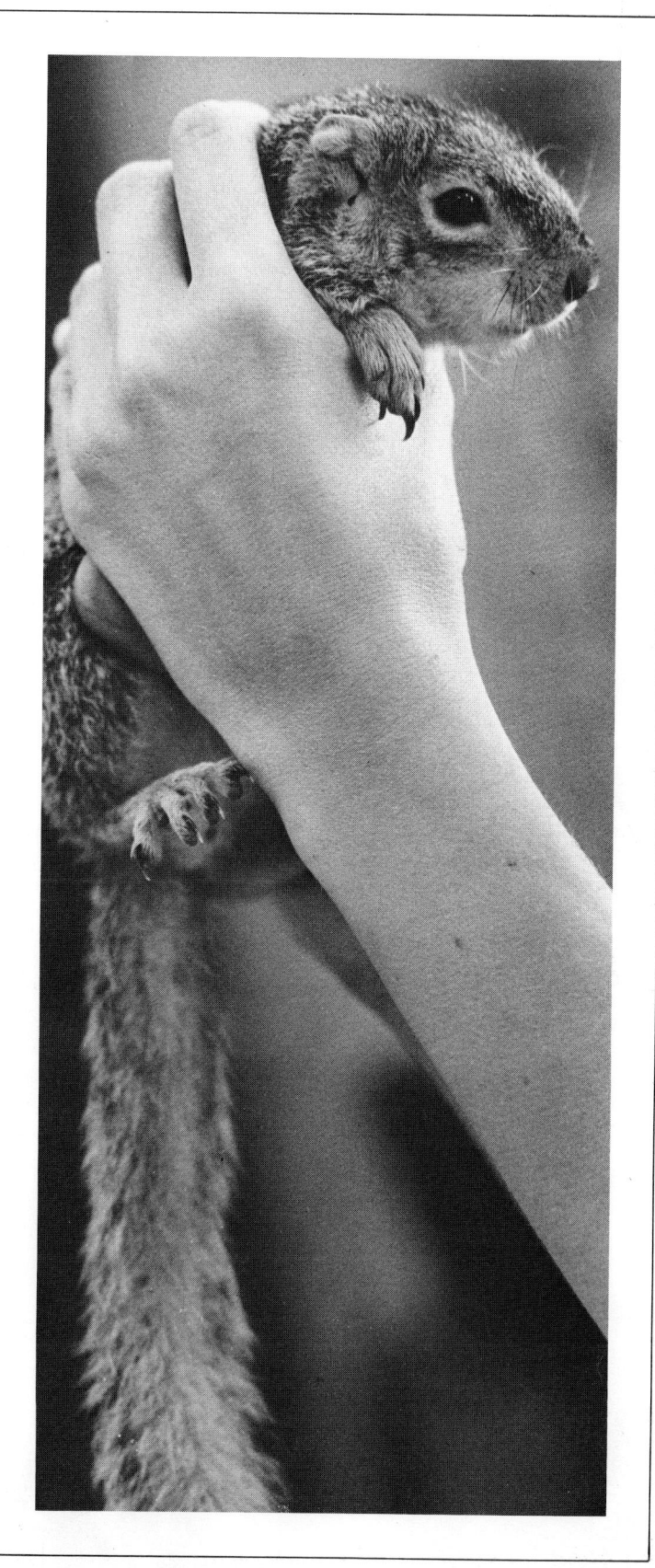

When Buffy returned to the shelter after visiting the school, his cage was empty. The other dog was gone. Her owner had claimed her. Now Buffy would be alone again.

The next day Max left the shelter too. He was adopted.

Officer Lee patted Buffy on the head. "I'm sure somebody will adopt you, too," she said.

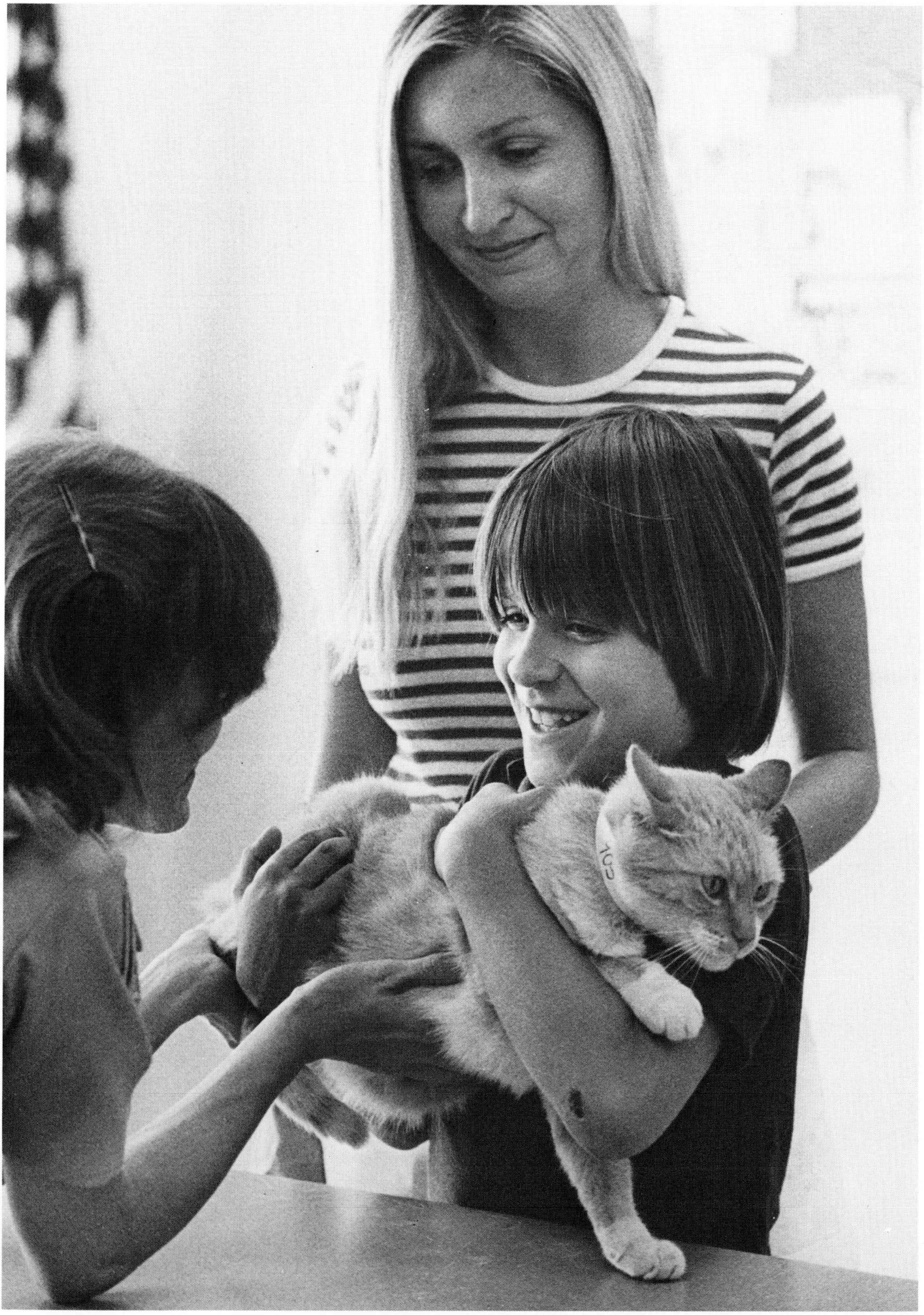

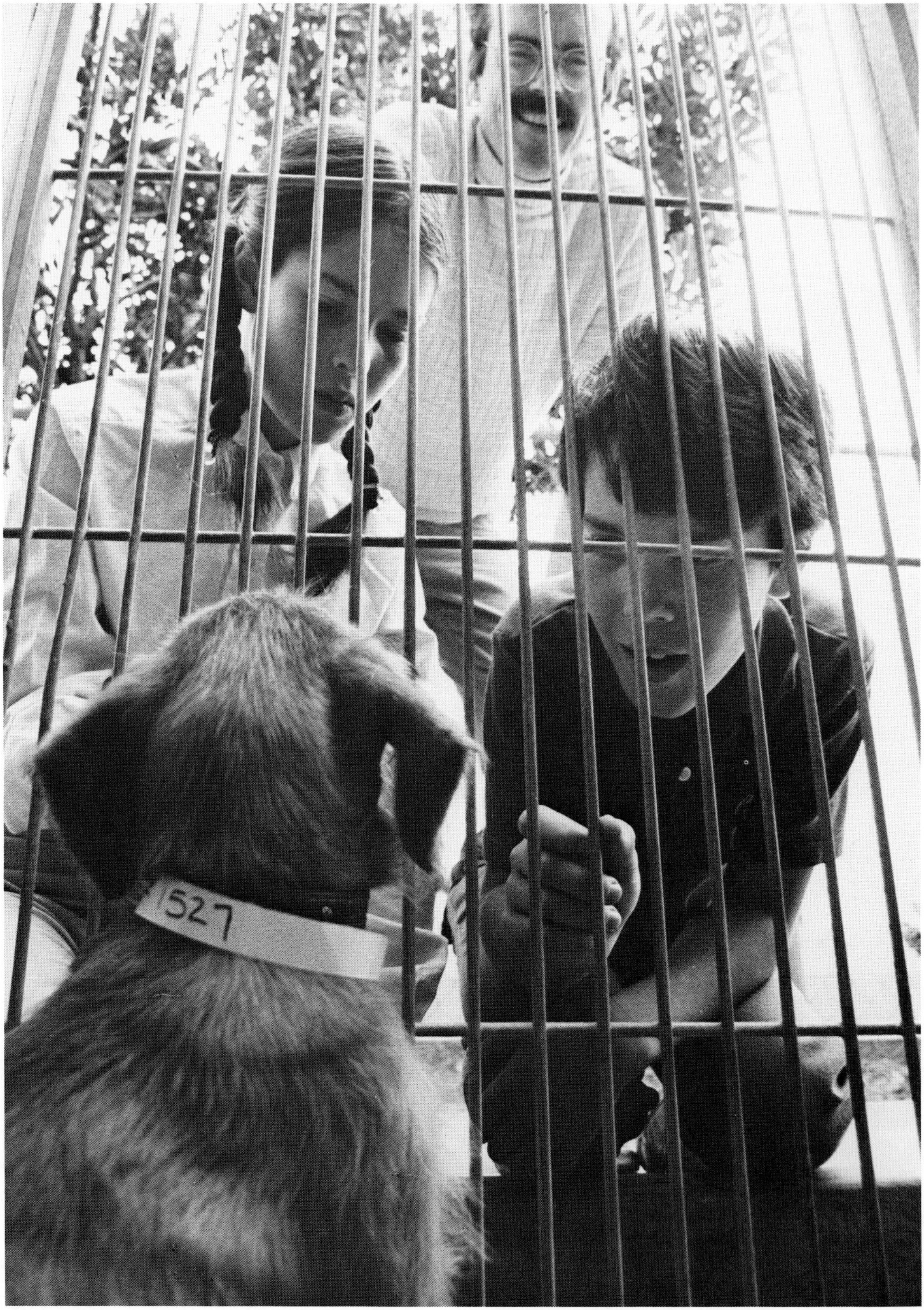
527

Then two children came to the shelter to find a new pet. They wanted one that was lively and fun to play with. They also wanted one that was small enough to exercise easily in their yard.

First they looked at the cats. Then they looked at the dogs. Finally they came to Buffy's cage. Buffy jumped up and wagged his tail. He pushed his wet nose through the bars.

The children decided that Buffy was just the pet they had been looking for. So, with the help of their father, they filled out the necessary forms to adopt Buffy. Then they gave Officer Lee the money for the adoption fee. Officer Lee gave them some information about puppy care.

Buffy looked as if he could hardly wait to go home with the children. "I can see you've already made friends," said Officer Lee. "Buffy was just waiting for some children like you. I know you will love him, play with him, and give him a good home. You and Buffy look like you will be very happy together."

Buffy and Max were lucky to be able to go to good homes. Unfortunately many animals at shelters are not adopted. Because there are not nearly enough homes for all the pets without them, many animals must be killed. No one at a shelter likes to do it, but when it is necessary, it is done quickly and painlessly.

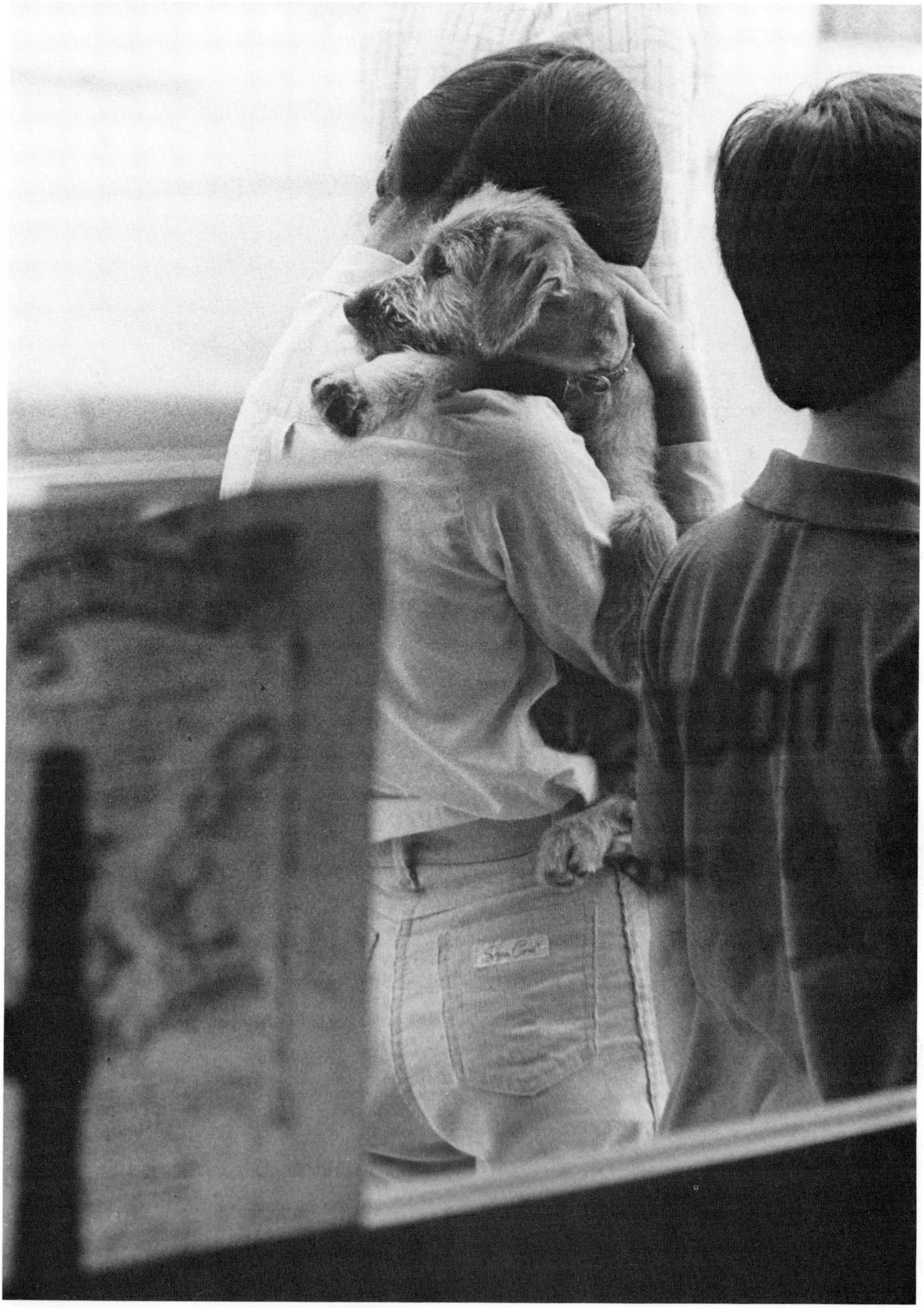

As more and more people learn to spay or neuter their pets, fewer unwanted animals will be born. Then shelters won't have too many animals to care for, and fewer animals will have to be killed.

People who work at animal shelters help keep animals in their community safe and healthy. And in every way they can, they try to see that as many pets as possible find good homes.